4 Ismay Hines, Shirley Moore, Norma Prime, Rita James,
Dawn Francis, Barbara Dellimore, Tina Gerrusi, Elaine Pensa,
Michelle Adelberg, Anna Scrivano, Angela Kamikawaji,
Olivia Rojas, Mattie Walker, Bunny Brown
—S.L.M.

First published in 2003 by Simply Read Books
501-5525 West Boulevard, Vancouver BC V6M 3W6

Colour separations by Scanlab

Caricature of Sean Moore by Gerry Fournier

Design by Robin Mitchell for Picnic

©2003 Sean Moore
Printed and bound in Italy by Grafiche AZ, Verona

Cataloguing in Publication Data

Moore,Sean,1976-
 Always run up the stairs/Sean Moore.

 ISBN 1-894965-05-1

 I.Title.
PS8676.O6155A88 2003   jC813'.6   C2003-911204-7

Always Run Up The Stairs

Sean Moore

There must be someone
who knows somewhere,
do those things really live
down there?

Just to be safe,
I always
run up the stairs.

There's really not
much need for fright,

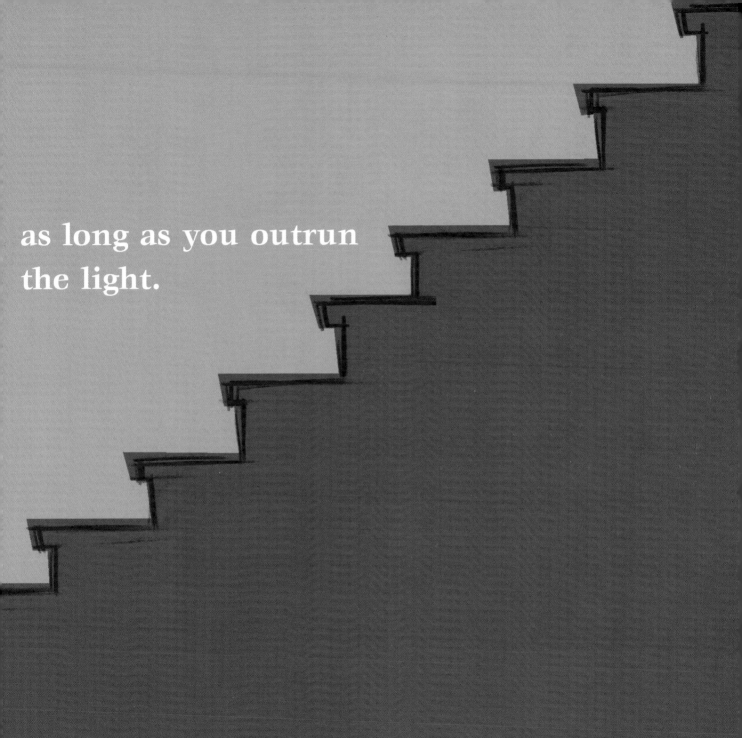

as long as you outrun
the light.

So just to be safe,
always run up the stairs.

You wouldn't dare
find out, I bet you.

You
never
know,
so
always

run
up
the
stairs.

Your parents won't believe you.

They'll only laugh and tease you.

Absolutely NO running
up the stairs.

Could they be wrong
or crazy, even?
Surely you'll be boiled
in stew and eaten.

My advice is—

always run up
the stairs.

I'm sure I heard
a noise down there
but I'll be brave.
No, I'm not scared.

A batch of
cookies
might just
work.

They won't eat me if I feed
them first.

After all, it's not
too dark downstairs.

We could play cards or
build laundry forts.

Play hide and seek,

Maybe it could be
really fun down there.

TiMe forbeD!

That can't be right.

I haven't gone,
but I still might.

Guess I'll wait and
go tomorrow, instead.

There must
be someone
who knows
somewhere,

Should I ask
the thing
that's hiding
under
my
bed?